Mucky Moose

written and illustrated by

Jonathan Allen

Macmillan Publishing Company
New York

Maxwell Macmillan International Publishing Group
New York   Oxford   Singapore   Sydney

In the tall, dark forests of the north, there lived a moose. His name was Mucky.

He was called Mucky because he *was* mucky—the muckiest, smelliest moose that ever lived.

Now, there was one muddy swamp in which every moose liked to wallow. But some parts were much too smelly and sludgy for most moose. These were Mucky's favorite wallowing places.

Mucky was so smelly that he attracted flies from miles away. They buzzed around his head in a big cloud. Birds perched on his antlers and snapped up the flies, while frogs sat on Mucky's nose and caught flies, too.

Mucky was so smelly that when he walked through the forest all the other animals kept out of his way—all except the skunks, that is. Skunks—as everyone knows—smell terrible, but no skunk was even half as smelly as Mucky. Whenever skunks met Mucky they were so impressed by his powerful smell that they gave him a round of applause.

In the forest there were lots of wolves. Everyone knows that wolves sometimes eat moose. When the biggest wolf in the forest heard about Mucky, the largest moose in the forest, he decided to eat him for his dinner.

"I'm the biggest wolf in the forest, and I'm *extra* hungry. So I'm going to eat the biggest moose in the forest!" he declared.

One morning, as Mucky was walking back from his daily,
smelly wallow—a cloud of flies buzzing around him, a couple
of birds on each antler—a huge wolf stepped out in front of him.

"I'm going to eat you for my dinner," he snarled. "I just thought you might like to know."

"How interesting," replied Mucky, "but I'm afraid that doesn't fit in with my plans."

The wolf was furious. No one had ever dared speak to him like that. He drew himself up to spring at Mucky.

Then, suddenly, the wind changed direction and blew Mucky's horrible smell right at him. Wolves have very sensitive noses. To a wolf, Mucky's smell was positively dangerous! The wolf let out a sort of choking noise and stopped in his tracks. He turned green, yellow—then green again. His toes curled, and he collapsed in a dead faint.

"Not hungry anymore?" Mucky chuckled as he continued on his way.

When the wolf recovered he was very angry indeed.
"I'll get that moose!" he growled.

A few days later, Mucky was strolling through the forest
when the wolf once more stepped out in front of him. This
time the wolf had a clothespin on his nose to protect him from
the moose's dangerous smell.

"I'b goig to ead you for by didder!" he cried as best he
could.

"You're going to do what?" asked Mucky.

"I'b goig to ead you for by didder!" yelled the wolf, his voice shaking with anger.

"I'm sorry, but I can't understand a word you're saying with that thing on your nose," Mucky replied.

The wolf spluttered—then snatched the clothespin off his nose.
"I said, I'm going to eat you for . . . YERK!"
As Mucky's smell hit him, the wolf turned green, then
yellow.

His ears curled up and his tail bent like a corkscrew. Then his legs crossed and he fell sideways in a faint even more deadly than before.

"Dear, oh dear!" said Mucky, as he stepped over him and continued his stroll through the forest. "Poor Wolfie's been taken ill. What a shame!"

It took the wolf a week to recover. He was beside himself with anger.

"I'll fix that smelly monster of a moose," he swore.

As he was walking back from his daily wallow, Mucky was
surprised to see the wolf step out in front of him yet again,
this time wearing a gas mask.

"Aha!" he cried in a muffled voice. "Got you now, Mucky
Moose! Prepare to be my dinner, and about time, too, I'd say."
The wolf drew himself up to his full height, ready to spring.
"Sorry, Mr. Wolf," said Mucky, "but how are you going to
bite me with that mask on?"

The wolf hadn't thought of that little detail. (Thinking was
not his strong point.)

"Naaaargh!" he yelled in frustration, tearing the gas mask
from his face. "Smell or no smell, I'm going to eat you now."

With a roar he leaped at Mucky, fangs bared.

When the smell hit him this time, he turned not only green, then yellow, but purple, too. His eyes crossed, his knees knocked together, and his tail revolved at high speed. Finally, his legs buckled, and he fell sideways in a dead faint—for the third time. Mucky shrugged and, shaking his head, stepped over the wolf's body, and continued on his way.

The wolf did not bother Mucky again after that. He left the forest forever—never to return. Changing his ways, he went to the nearest city to become a guide wolf for the blind.

The other wolves sensibly kept away from Mucky, who just went on as he always had, wallowing happily in the smelliest parts of the swamp he could find and talking to his friends, the birds, frogs, and skunks.